This book belongs to

....

#TinyOwlBloom

Copyright © Tiny Owl Publishing 2020
Text © Anne Booth 2020
Illustrations © Robyn Wilson-Owen 2020

First published in the UK in 2020 by
Tiny Owl Publishing, London

www.tinyowl.co.uk

A catalogue record for this book is available from the British Library.

ISBN 978-1-910328-44-6

Printed in Czech Republic

Bloom

Anne Booth   Robyn Wilson-Owen

TINY OWL

There was once a beautiful flower which grew under
the window of a big house, and a little girl who loved it.

Every morning, on her way to school with her brother,
the little girl would visit the flower.

She would look at its beautiful petals, drink in its sweet smell, and wonder at the smoothness of its leaves and at their colour and shape.

'Good morning, beautiful flower,' she would say.

'I think you're wonderful. Thank you for being here for us. I love you,' and she would go to school happy.

One morning, the man living in the big house woke up
early and heard someone talking to his flower.

He looked out of his window and saw the little girl.

'How dare you talk to MY flower?' he shouted.
'Go away and never come near my flower again!'

The little girl and her brother didn't like being
shouted at, so they went to school another way.

The next day, when the sun rose,
the flower did not open.

And every day after that it stayed tight shut.
The man was furious and sent for his gardener.

'What is the matter with my flower?'
he demanded.

'Is it getting enough water?'

'Yes,' said the gardener. 'I water it every morning and evening.'

'Well, you're obviously not doing it properly,'
said the man crossly.
'I can see I am just going to have to do it myself.'

And so every morning
he got up and watered
the flower, and every
evening before he
went to bed he
watered the flower.

But it still refused
to open.

'Maybe it needs more shade?' said the man.
'The sun is very hot in the middle of the day.'

'I have made sure it has plenty of shade,'
said the gardener.

But the man said, **'well, you're obviously not doing it
properly. I can see I am just going to have to do it myself.'**

So every day, when the sun was at its highest, he took
his umbrella and shaded the flower from the heat.

But it still didn't open.

He watered
the flower in
the morning

and shaded it from
the midday sun

and watered it
again just before
he went to bed.

The man began to talk to it. He told it how wonderful he was,

how lucky it was to be his flower, and how important his job was.

But it still didn't open.

He told it all about his problems,
how busy he was, and the fact
that nobody liked him.

He complained about how his gardener was rubbish,
how if he didn't do everything, nothing got done
properly, and how lonely he felt.

He ordered it to bloom
for him to cheer him up.

The unhappy man called the gardener to him again.

'Before you say ANYTHING,' said the gardener,
'I don't know what the matter is. All I know is that the
flower hasn't opened since you sent away the little
school girl who passed by it every morning.'

'What did she do that I don't do?'
said the man crossly.

'Well, she used to talk to it every day,'
said the gardener.

'**That can't be it,**' said the man.

'I talk to it every morning, at midday and before
I go to bed, and what I can say must be MUCH
better than anything a little girl could say.'

The man thought
and thought.

'I can see I am just going to have to ask that child to come back. Maybe she has some magic words which make the flower bloom.'

So he went to the school gate
and waited for the little girl
and her brother to arrive.

'My flower stopped blooming after you left,'
said the man to the little girl.

'Poor flower,' said the little girl.

'I've watered it and sheltered it and talked to it every day, but it still
won't open,' and a tear rolled down his cheek.

'What do you say to it?' said the little girl, and her brother passed the man a hankie.

'Well,' said the man, blowing his nose.

'I tell it how important I am and how lucky it is to be in my garden. I tell it how miserable I am. I tell it how horrible everybody else is, and I order it to bloom to cheer me up. But it doesn't work.'

'Well,' said the little girl.

'Why don't you tell it
how wonderful it is,
thank it for being there,
and how much you love it?
That's what I always did.'

So the man ran home to his flower and said

'You are wonderful.'

And as he said the words, he realised
for the first time how truly wonderful
the flower was.

'I'm so lucky you grow in my garden,'
he said, and as he said it he realised
how truly lucky he was, and how he
hadn't ever really looked at his flower
properly, and how much he longed to
see it and smell its perfume again.

'**I love you so much,**' said the man
at last, and as he said it, his own
heart filled with love.

And the flower bloomed.

About the Authors

Anne Booth

Robyn Wilson-Owen

Anne Booth lives in a little village and is lucky to know lovely people who are very kind to her and make her bloom. She has a very kind husband, four children and two very friendly dogs, and she has loving friends in and out of her village. Every day she thinks how lucky she is and how beautiful they all are and how much she loves them. It makes her very happy whenever she says that out loud back to them and about them, so that they can bloom too! She hopes the readers of this story will bloom and help others to bloom as well! She feels blooming lucky that her agent is Anne Clark and that her book has been published by Tiny Owl and illustrated by Robyn Wilson-Owen!

Robyn Wilson-Owen was a set, costume, and puppet designer for a long time before she started illustrating. Now she uses dip pens, ink, and colouring pencils to create her work. She spends a lot of time drawing the world around her in her sketchbook, which is where she finds most of her ideas.